THIS BLOOMSBURY BOOK

BELONGS TO

....

Sharp Teeth Mountains

Dog Bowl Lake

Whiskers
Cove

Wag Island

Bone Dry Desert

✗

Deep Paw Swamp

To Nicola, my granddaughter

First published in Great Britain in 2007 by Bloomsbury Publishing Plc
36 Soho Square, London, W1D 3QY

Text and illustrations copyright © 2007 Michael Terry

A CIP catalogue record of this book is available from the British Library

ISBN 978 0 7475 8895 5

Printed and bound in China

1 3 5 7 9 10 8 6 4 2

All papers used by Bloomsbury Publishing are natural, recyclable products
made from wood grown in well-managed forests. The manufacturing processes
conform to the environmental regulations of the country of origin.

Captain Wag the Pirate Dog

Michael Terry

BLOOMSBURY
CHILDREN'S
BOOKS

Captain Wag was a wily old pirate who had sailed the seven seas. And Captain Wag was a very happy pirate, because . . .

. . . in his paws he held a map.
A TREASURE MAP!

'I have to find this treasure,' Captain Wag thought.
'But first I need two shipmates.'

Captain Wag went to meet his old friends One-Eye Jack and
Old Scratch.

'Take a look at this, me hearties,' said Captain Wag in a
low growl. 'Will you sail with me to find this treasure?
Treasure fit to gladden the heart of any dog!
It won't be easy and there will be many a danger
on the way, but there will be a share
in the treasure for you.'

'Are you with me, shipmates?'
'Aye, we're with you, Captain Wag!' shouted One-Eye Jack and
Old Scratch. 'When do we set sail?'
'TOMORROW, my shipmates!' cried Captain Wag.

They struggled through storms
with mountainous waves
and lashing rain.

They fought with giant sea monsters.

They battled with raging thirst in the hot tropics.

But more trouble was brewing . . .

Pirate Ginger Tom, the fiercest
cat on the high seas, had heard
about Captain Wag's treasure
map from one of his spies.
He immediately set sail . . .
and, after a fierce battle,
captured Captain Wag
and his shipmates!

'Wag, you old sea dog, give us that treasure map,'
hissed Pirate Ginger Tom.
'Not on your life, you old catfish,' growled
Captain Wag . . . and threw the map overboard!

'Now you will have to take us with you if you want to find the treasure,' said Captain Wag defiantly. 'Curses on you, Wag,' cried Pirate Ginger Tom.

After many days' sailing, Pirate Ginger Tom and his crew were getting impatient. Then Captain Wag cried, 'Land ahoy!' There on the horizon lay the treasure island.

'Right, Wag,' demanded Ginger Tom. 'Show us where the treasure is, and be quick about it.'

'You will find it ten paces north from that rock,' said Captain Wag with a wily grin. 'And I hope you will be happy with it.'

It took many hours for Pirate Ginger Tom and his crew
to dig out the treasure chest. But when they heaved open
the lid, they were not happy – not happy at all!

'BISCUITS AND BONES!' hissed the enraged cats. 'Nothing but dog biscuits and mouldy old bones!' They stamped back to their ship in a fearful temper.

'Just as I said, lads!' cried Captain Wag. 'Treasure fit to gladden the heart of any dog!'

And Captain Wag, One-Eye Jack and Old Scratch ate heartily and laughed long at Pirate Ginger Tom and his luckless pirate cats.

Sharp Teeth Mountains

Dog Bowl Lake

Whiskers Cove

Bone Dry Desert

Wag Island

X

Deep Paw Swamp

Also by Michael Terry

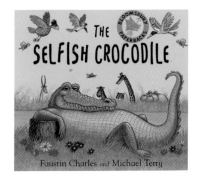

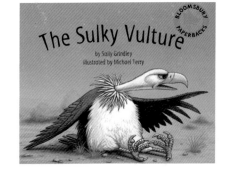

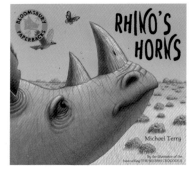

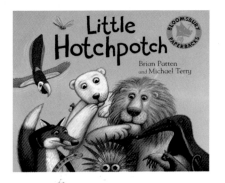

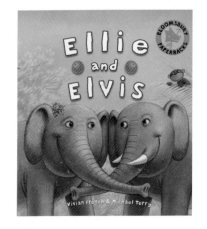

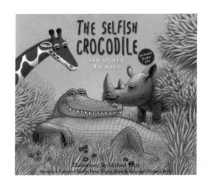

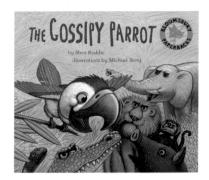